Ou
New B

Illustrations by
Amelia Rosato

EGMONT
(children's book)

First published in Great Britain 2000 by Egmont Children's Books Limited
239 Kensington High Street, London W8 6SA
Illustrated by Amelia Rosato
Text by Laura Dollin. Designed by Suzanne Cocks.
Copyright © 2000 Egmont Children's Books Limited
ISBN 0 7497 4186 4
Printed in Italy

1 3 5 7 9 10 8 6 4 2

Dad's cleaning the cot.
It's dusty from the cupboard.

It's not very long until the baby is here.

Mum's tummy is **SO** big I can't fit on her lap!

"You will soon," says Mum, "when the baby is here."

"Be a good girl for Grandma," says Dad to me.
When they come home again,
the baby will be here.

The baby is called Sammy and he makes a lot of noise. It's never very quiet now the baby is here.

He cries and he yells

and he eats
and he smells.

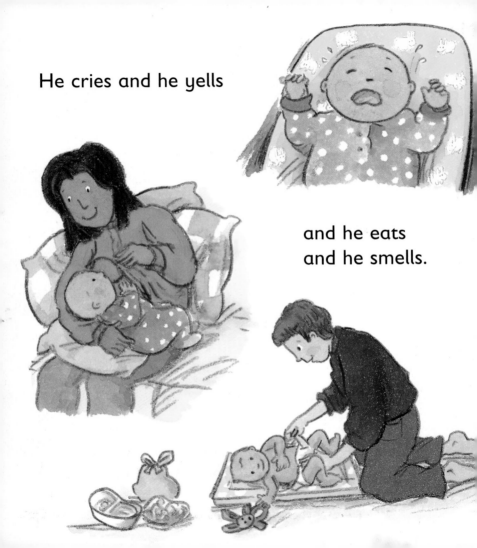

Mum is falling asleep,

Dad is cooking the tea.

When I turn upside-down
Or I wear a big hat,
Nobody notices **me** doing that!

It's the baby, the baby, the baby again,
"Mummy, how long
must the baby live here?"

Perhaps I could hide him in a secret place ...

... and pretend that the baby is not really here.

Perhaps he'll go away if I make a scary face ...

... but the baby seems to like it,
and is very much still here.

So I tickle and cuddle him, waggle his toes,
I bounce up and down with him, wiggle his nose.

And he giggles and giggles
and chuckles out loud ...

Oh it's so much more fun now the baby is here!